The Rescue Princesses
The Star Bracelet

Lily lifted Fudge out of the bag and sat down with the joey on her lap. The little kangaroo wriggled more than ever! Lily put the baby kangaroo on the floor and Fudge did a few wobbly jumps across the room...

Have you read?

The Secret Promise

The Wishing Pearl

The Moonlit Mystery

The Stolen Crystals

The Snow Jewel

The Magic Rings

The Lost Gold

The Shimmering Stone

The Silver Locket

The Ice Diamond

The Rainbow Opal

The Golden Shell

Look out for:

The Enchanted Ruby

The Amber Necklace

The Rescue Princesses
The Star Bracelet

Paula Harrison

nosy crow

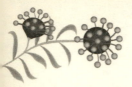

First published in the UK in 2018 by Nosy Crow Ltd
The Crow's Nest, 14 Baden Place,
Crosby Row, London SE1 1YW

Nosy Crow and associated logos are trademarks and/or registered
trademarks of Nosy Crow Ltd

Text © Paula Harrison, 2018
Cover illustration © Sharon Tancredi, 2018
Interior illustrations © Artful Doodlers, 2018

The right of Paula Harrison to be identified as the author of this work
has been asserted by her in accordance with the Copyright, Designs
and Patents Act, 1988

Printed and bound in Great Britain by Clays Ltd, Elcograf S.p.A.

Papers used by Nosy Crow are made from wood grown in
sustainable forests.

ISBN: 978 0 85763 987 5

www.nosycrow.com

For everyone at the Kangaroo
Sanctuary in Alice Springs

Chapter One

The Pony-Roo

Princess Lily slipped down the stairs like a ninja. She missed out the creaky step near the bottom and reached the palace hallway without making a sound. Tucking her blonde hair behind her ears, she stopped to listen. Her mum, Queen Caroline, was talking to Lady Hamilton in the parlour. Lily tiptoed towards the front door and silently put on her shoes.

CRASH! She stumbled into a coat stand, knocking it to the floor.

1

Queen Caroline appeared in the doorway, smiling. "Are you all right, Lily? If you're playing outside make sure you're back for lunch, won't you?"

"I will!" Lily smiled back, but her shoulders sank as she crossed the palace garden. She'd tried and tried to get better at ninja moves. Today she'd crept halfway round the palace without anyone spotting her. But as soon as she thought she was improving, she knocked something over or tripped and fell down. The moves were such an important part of being a Rescue Princess – so she had to keep trying! Her new friends Scarlett and Zina would be here later and she wanted to show them how much she'd practised.

The sun came out from behind a big cloud, shining down on Saronga Palace with its long row of golden turrets.

Lily cheered up as she thought about seeing her friends again. The three princesses had met two months ago at Scarlett's birthday party. Together they had rescued a baby otter and stopped a thief from stealing lots of precious jewels.

Scarlett had told the other girls about her cousin who, along with some friends, had made a secret promise to always save animals in danger. They called themselves the Rescue Princesses and they used teamwork and ninja moves, *and* they had magic jewels to help them. After hearing about it, Lily had decided that they should become Rescue Princesses straightaway!

A few weeks later, Scarlett had sent Lily and Zina magic rings that she'd made with her jewel-making tools. Each one was a beautiful heart shape and when the girls pressed the jewels they could speak to each other secretly. Scarlett's jewel was a shining red ruby and Zina's was a sparkling diamond. Lily's jewel was a deep-blue sapphire and she loved hers best of all!

Lily smiled. She was so glad her mum had invited the other girls to stay. She pressed the sapphire on her ring and waited for the jewel to light up. "Is anyone there?" she whispered. "Can you hear me?"

"Yes, we're here." Scarlett's voice floated out of the jewel. "We're on our way to your palace right now."

"Hooray – you're early!" Lily hopped up and down. "I'll see you soon."

"Bye, Lily! See you soon!" Zina and Scarlett called back, and then the jewel went dark again.

Lily ran all the way to the royal stables, excitement bubbling inside her.

Ten golden wattle trees covered with bright-yellow flowers lined the path and a row of royal bluebells nodded in the breeze. Saronga Palace had one of the finest gardens in the whole of Estaland. Lily really hoped her new friends would like it.

Skipping into the stables, Lily stopped beside her favourite pony's stall. "Hello, Sandy! How are you?" A pony with a golden coat came over and let Lily stroke her nose. "Good girl! Would you like a sugar lump?"

As the pony nibbled the sugar, Lily spotted another animal in the next-door stall and leaned over to get a better look. The stall next to Sandy's was usually empty. She was surprised to see a small reddish-brown kangaroo lying against a bale of hay.

"Hello! What are you doing in there?"

said Lily, laughing.

"That's Hoppley." Matt, the stable-hand, came in carrying a saddle. "I've been taking care of him ever since he got thrown from his mother's pouch when he was a very young joey. He's nearly big enough to look after himself now and this is the first time I've let him out to explore the palace garden."

"Hi, Hoppley! You look pretty comfortable there." Lily smiled. She was used to seeing kangaroos in the fields and woods near the palace. Sometimes they even hopped up the palace drive and into the garden, but she'd never seen one in the stables before.

Hoppley's ears twitched and he hopped up and down the stall.

"I think he's in that stall because he's decided he's a pony!" said Matt.

"If he's a kangaroo AND a pony that

makes him a pony-roo!" said Lily. "How did you know what to do when he was left behind by his mother?"

Matt sat down on a bale of hay. "I knew he should stay in a pouch so I stitched a sack into the right shape and put him inside. Since then I've been feeding him special milk from a baby's bottle but I don't think he needs it any more."

Lily nodded. She wished the kangaroo still needed the milk. She would've loved to have fed him.

"I'll be able help more joeys once I open my kangaroo sanctuary," added Matt.

Lily nodded. She'd talked to Matt about his plans for the sanctuary lots of times. Matt was such an expert on kangaroos!

The little kangaroo jumped up and sniffed at the stable door. "Here you go, Hoppley." Lily opened the door wider and the little kangaroo bounded out just as a car rolled up the palace drive.

"Those must be your visitors, Princess Lily," said Matt. "I'll get the suitcases."

"Thank you, Matt." Lily ran forward, nearly slipping on the gravel.

The car rolled into the yard with two girls waving madly inside. Scarlett was the first to jump out, her black curls bouncing on her shoulders. Then Zina climbed out, smiling shyly.

"We're here at last!" Scarlett noticed Hoppley bouncing out of the stable yard. "You didn't tell us you had a pet kangaroo, Lily."

"I don't!" said Lily, laughing. "That's Hoppley. Matt looked after him when he was little but now he's bigger and ready to hop around on his own."

Matt, who was taking the suitcases out of the car boot, smiled at the girls and gave a little bow.

"You have really interesting animals here," said Zina. "And it's so warm too."

"You'll probably see lots of kangaroos while you're staying with me," Lily told them. "They're a very common animal in our kingdom."

"I wish I could hop like that!" Scarlett tried to copy Hoppley's jumps.

Soon the princesses were all leaping around like kangaroos until they began giggling too much to jump any more.

"Matt's going to start up a sanctuary for kangaroos that need looking after," said Lily.

Matt nodded. "Although it could be a few months before the sanctuary opens, Your Highness. I'd love to start sooner but I don't have enough money yet."

Lily bit her lip. "But in the meantime there could be lots of baby kangaroos that need help."

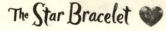

"Maybe we could raise some money for the sanctuary," said Zina.

"We could do a sponsored jump!" said Scarlett excitedly.

"Or we could bake lots of cakes and set up a cake stall at the palace gates." Lily's eyes lit up. "We'd have to ask my mum but I bet she'd say yes!"

"I love making cakes!" said Scarlett, and Zina nodded.

"It's very kind of you all but you don't have to go to a lot of bother," began Matt.

"We don't mind!" said Lily. She looked round at the other girls. Zina was smiling and Scarlett gave a wink. She knew what they were thinking. Raising money for a kangaroo sanctuary was just the kind of thing the Rescue Princesses would love to do!

Chapter Two

Lady Hamilton's Car

Lily dashed into the palace and threw
open the parlour door. "The other
princesses have arrived!" she told her
mum. "And guess what?"

Queen Caroline looked up in surprise.
"Lily, don't rush in like that! What will
people think?" She glanced at her guest,
Lady Hamilton, who frowned as she took
a sip from her china teacup.

The other princesses clattered in
after Lily, still out of breath from their

kangaroo jumping.

"Sorry!" Lily shook some hay off her dress and tried to remember the proper thing to say. "Um … here is Princess Scarlett from the Kingdom of Deronda, and this is Princess Zina from the Kingdom of Ramova."

Both the princesses came forward to say hello and Zina dropped a graceful curtsy.

"Thanks so much for inviting us here, Queen Caroline," said Scarlett. "Your palace is lovely."

The queen smiled. "That's very kind of you! I'm so pleased that you've come to stay with us. I know Lily's been looking forward to seeing you. Now, it's important to remember that dinner is at half past five. Lily will show you where your rooms are and if there's anything else you need, please just ask. Let me see … what else do I need to tell you?"

Lily fidgeted with her sleeve. She hoped her mum would stop talking so that she could ask about the cake sale.

There was a knock at the parlour door and a heavy-looking man with a round face came in. "Good afternoon, Your Majesty. Good afternoon, Your Ladyship." He bowed to the queen and Lady Hamilton. "You asked to be picked up at eleven, Your Ladyship, and the car is ready. I'll wait outside."

"Thank you, Delby." Lady Hamilton rose from her chair, wrapping a purple shawl around her thin shoulders. "Well, I hope you will show these girls what it means to be an Estaland princess," she said to Lily. "In my day we practised curtsying so low that our knees would touch the floor."

Lily wasn't sure what to say. She couldn't imagine why anyone would

14

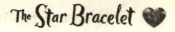

want to curtsy like that!

"We just met a kangaroo and we think he's lovely!" Scarlett suddenly burst out.

"What's that?" Lady Hamilton's eyes bulged. "You have a kangaroo here?"

"There was one in the stable yard," Lily explained quickly. "Actually, that's what we came to ask about." She turned to her mum. "Matt wants to set up the kangaroo sanctuary soon but he doesn't have enough money. So we thought we could have a cake sale to help him." She clasped her hands together. "Please can we? I promise we'll do all the cooking and clearing up ourselves."

"That's a good idea," the queen smiled. "Yes, I don't see why not. As long as you ask Cook to help you with the oven."

"And where is this kangaroo place going to be?" asked Lady Hamilton, frowning deeply.

"It will be quite close to where you live actually," replied the queen. "I gave permission for Matt to use some royal land. There's a nice field with lots of room for the animals."

Lady Hamilton's face darkened like a rain cloud. "There are too many animal parks these days. They spread muck and dirt, and if the creatures can't look after themselves then I don't see why people should pay money so that they can be pampered."

Scarlett went red. "I don't think that's fair—" she began, but Lily nudged her and she fell silent.

"Let me see you out, Sarah," the queen said hurriedly. "It was so nice of you to visit and I hope you'll come again." She ushered Lady Hamilton from the room.

The princesses exchanged looks once the queen and Lady Hamilton had gone.

"That lady wasn't very nice," said Scarlett, frowning. "I can't believe she doesn't like animal parks."

"It was really mean of her!" cried Lily. "But the good thing is we're allowed to do the cake sale and that will raise the money the sanctuary needs."

"We should draw some posters and put them up outside the palace gate," said Zina.

"That's a great idea!" Lily's eyes lit up. "Then everyone will know when to come. I've got lots of paint in the cupboard. I just need to find the painting aprons." She hurried out to the hallway and opened a tall cupboard crammed with paintbrushes and glitter.

Zina crouched down beside her. "You have lots of art things, Lily! Would these be good for the posters?" She drew out some extra-large sheets of paper.

"Those would be great! Shall we do one poster each?" Lily reached behind the paint pots. "I've found the aprons."

There was a loud revving noise outside. Lily looked through the front window and saw her mum wave to Lady Hamilton as the car drove away. Then the queen walked round the corner towards the stables.

"That lady has a very posh car," said Scarlett. "Oh look, there's the kangaroo again. What was his name, Lily?"

"Hoppley!" Lily counted out three aprons before taking some paintbrushes.

"That one's too big to be Hoppley," said Zina. "And look, she's got a baby!"

The girls all rushed to the window. Hopping across the palace lawn was a large kangaroo with a baby peeping out of its pouch.

"Aw, that's really sweet!" cooed Zina.

"How long do their mothers carry them around like that?"

"Quite a long time. The little babies are called joeys." Lily frowned. The mother kangaroo was bounding towards the palace gate just as Lady Hamilton's car drew closer. Surely the driver would see the animal and stop?

The driver shouted something through the car window and beeped his horn at the kangaroo. Then the car sped up.

"That car's going too fast!" Zina's eyes widened. "I hope the kangaroo doesn't jump in front of it!"

The driver honked his horn even louder. The kangaroo turned sharply, jumping into the bushes. As it swung round, the little joey fell from its pouch and tumbled on to the grass.

"The baby's fallen out!" gasped Scarlett. "The mother kangaroo will go back for it, won't she?"

The kangaroo bounded away through the bushes.

"She's too scared by that horrible beeping," said Zina.

Lady Hamilton's driver sounded the horn one more time before the car swept through the gate and out on to the road. The big kangaroo sprang out of the bushes and jumped right over the palace wall.

"Wait – come back!" called Lily, running out of the front door and down the palace steps.

But the mother kangaroo had gone and her baby was left all alone, trembling on the grass.

Chapter Three

The Little Kangaroo

The three princesses ran down the palace drive, their eyes fixed on the little bundle of fur left on the grass. Zina, who was the fastest runner, reached the joey first. The creature was lying crumpled up, squeaking softly. Lily and Zina knelt down beside it.

"You poor thing!" said Lily. "It must be so scary suddenly bouncing out of your mother's pouch like that."

The joey tried to stand up but its legs

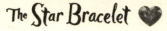

were too wobbly and it flopped down on to the grass again.

"What shall we do?" Scarlett pushed back her dark hair. "We can't leave her here and it doesn't look like the mother's coming back."

"Matt told me once that the mothers never come back, and this little joey looks too young to survive on her own," said Lily. "We should take her to Matt – he'll know what to do." She gathered the baby in her arms and set off across the garden.

The joey squeaked again and wriggled. Lily stroked the animal's soft fur and whispered soothingly, "Don't worry! We'll look after you."

The princesses hurried past the line of golden wattle trees into the stable yard. But the yard was empty and the car that had brought the girls from the airport had gone.

"Matt? Where are you?" called Lily.

Scarlett dashed into the stables and came out a moment later. "Matt's not here but that other kangaroo, Hoppley, is sleeping on a bale of hay."

Lily passed the little kangaroo to Scarlett. "I'll ask inside. Maybe he's having his break." She hurried down the path and through the back door, and found Cook Ingram chopping carrots in the kitchen.

"Hello, Princess Lily," said Cook. "Where are those friends of yours? I thought they'd arrived."

"They're just outside," replied Lily. "I'm looking for Matt. Have you seen him?"

"He's gone, I'm afraid." Cook set down the vegetable knife. "He's doing some more work at the new kangaroo sanctuary – mending the fences and so on. He won't be back till tomorrow."

"Oh!" Lily bit her lip.

Cook studied her. "Is everything all right, my dear? Shall I get you all some milk and cookies?"

"Yes, please! I'll be back for them in a minute." Lily led her friends to her room and brought up Cook's milk and cookies on a tray. She explained to Scarlett and Zina that Matt had gone away. "We're Rescue Princesses," she added. "So we'll just have to look after the little joey ourselves."

"I'd much rather we did it ourselves!" Scarlett held the little kangaroo even tighter. "We can give her some milk and keep her warm."

Lily fiddled with her hair. "I'm a bit worried because Matt told me he fed Hoppley some special milk. So I'm not sure if ordinary milk is the best thing for kangaroos."

25

"We have to feed her something." Scarlett stroked the animal's soft ears. "At least it'll only be for one day."

"That's true!" said Lily. "I think I've seen a squeezy bottle in the kitchen that we can put the milk in."

"What shall we call her?" said Zina eagerly. "Maybe she could be Bouncy!"

"She's got such lovely brown fur," said Lily. "So why don't we call her Fudge? It just feels right!"

The little kangaroo gave a squeak as if she agreed.

While Zina had a turn at cuddling the little animal, Lily and Scarlett crept downstairs to find the squeezy bottle. Then they poured some of their milk into the bottle and fed it to Fudge. The animal sucked hard, holding the sides of the bottle with her little paws. At last her ears grew floppy and her eyes began to close.

"We need a pouch to keep her in," whispered Zina. "What shall we do?"

Lily thought hard. "Matt said he sewed material together to make a pouch. Maybe I've got something in here that would do." She rushed over to her wardrobe.

At the bottom, among all the shoes, was a yellow cloth bag. Lily picked it up and showed it to the others. "How about this? I think it's just the right size."

"It's nice and soft!" Scarlett touched the bag. "And maybe we could pad it with something to make it cosy."

Lily searched through her drawers and pulled out some pairs of stripy socks. "These are soft and comfortable."

Zina held the joey tight while the other girls stuffed the socks into the bottom of the cloth bag. Then Lily carefully lifted the sleeping animal out of Zina's arms

and slid her into the bag. She hung the
bag from the handle of her wardrobe
door. The joey woke up and started to
wriggle.

"Shh! It's all right." Lily swayed the bag
very gently.

"How about a lullaby?" Scarlett began
singing softly. "Go to sleep, go to sleep,
go to sleep little Fudge…"

The others joined in and Lily carried on
rocking the cloth bag very carefully until
Fudge fell fast asleep.

"We should make those posters for
the cake sale right now," whispered
Lily. "Fudge might need a place at the
kangaroo sanctuary and without more
money Matt can't even open it."

Lily led Zina and Scarlett downstairs
to fetch the paint and paper. Then she
cleared everything off her desk to make
room for them to start.

"I'm going to make a 'Please buy our cakes' sign," decided Scarlett.

"I'm drawing a mother kangaroo with a baby in her pouch. Then everyone can see what we're raising money for," said Zina, concentrating hard.

"They're going to look brilliant!" beamed Lily, squeezing glue on to her poster and shaking gold glitter all over it.

Half an hour later, the princesses had finished their posters. Each one was very different but together they looked amazing. A fluttery feeling grew in Lily's stomach as she left them out to dry. With these colourful posters, they were sure to get lots of people coming to their cake sale. Then they would raise plenty of money for lost kangaroos everywhere!

Chapter Four

Ninja Trouble

Lily gathered up the paint pots and brushes. "We'd better go and wash these."

Zina nodded. "We should fetch some more milk as well. Fudge might be hungry when she wakes up."

"We could get some extra cookies from the kitchen too," said Scarlett, picking up the last biscuit on the plate.

"And I can show you my new ninja moves on the way," Lily said eagerly.

"I've been practising a lot."

The girls crept out quietly so that they didn't wake Fudge. They washed the paintbrushes and pots in the bathroom sink before hurrying downstairs.

Lily led the way, stopping every few steps to check if anyone was coming. "This is how I've been practising ninja moves!" she whispered to the others.

"Remember – keep low!" hissed Scarlett. "You have to try and stay invisible."

Lily reached the bottom of the stairs and crouched behind the coat stand. Peeking round the parlour door, she saw her mum reading a book.

The palace was quiet and the only sounds were parrots squawking in the garden and the distant neighing of a horse. Lily hesitated. It would be tricky returning the paint things to the cupboard without being heard.

Zina nodded encouragingly, so Lily crept past the parlour door. She ducked through the doorway into the dining room just as Cook came down the corridor. Cook passed by without seeing her and Lily breathed a sigh of relief. She really wanted to prove to the others that she could be a perfect ninja princess.

Tiptoeing out of the dining room, she went to the cupboard and opened the door.

CRASH! Five tins of crayons slid off the shelf on to the ground. Lily jumped and dropped her paint pots, making a second crash.

"Oh it's you, Lily." Her mum appeared in the parlour doorway. "What's going on? Are you all right?"

"Yes, sorry! I just dropped some things." Lily gathered up the tins and pots. Zina and Scarlett rushed to help her tidy up.

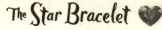

"Have fun, girls! Don't forget dinner is at half past five." Her mum disappeared back into the parlour.

Lily's cheeks turned red. "It's no good! I try to be quiet but something always goes wrong."

"But you were doing so well until you reached the cupboard," Zina told her.

"That's what happens every time." Lily sighed. "I feel like I'm finally managing to do the ninja moves properly but then I trip or knock something over."

"You just need a bit of training." Scarlett shoved the last of the paint pots and glitter into the cupboard. "Watch me! I'll creep into the kitchen and get some cookies without Cook seeing. Then you can copy me."

"All right." Lily waited with Zina, as Scarlett sneaked down the corridor.

Cook was humming to herself as she

35

washed up at the sink. Scarlett tiptoed past her, dipping behind a cupboard as Cook turned round to get a tea towel. Then she opened the cupboard without making a sound, took out the cookies and slipped back into the corridor.

"That was amazing!" whispered Lily. "Cook didn't see or hear a thing."

Scarlett grinned. "It's just about being quick and finding a good hiding place when you need one. Now you try! See if you can fetch Fudge's milk without anyone seeing."

"All right!" Lily's heart beat faster as she peered round the kitchen door. Cook was drying the dishes. Now was the perfect time!

Dashing across the kitchen, she pulled the fridge door open very carefully. The milk was right at the back behind a large bowl of trifle. Cook was still turned

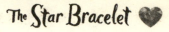

away looking out of the window as she dried the dishes. Lily's hand shook as she poured some of the milk into a jug. She'd nearly done it!

She put the milk back and closed the fridge without a sound but when she turned to go, her shoe squeaked on the tiled floor.

Cook swung round. "Hello, Princess Lily! I didn't hear you come in. Are the other girls still thirsty?"

Lily looked down at the milk jug. She wanted to tell Cook about the joey but what if she didn't approve of them bringing Fudge indoors?

Cook studied her. "What is it? I won't be cross, I promise."

Zina and Scarlett ran into the room. "We're looking after something upstairs," began Scarlett.

"It's a joey that fell out of its mother's

pouch," explained Lily. "We're looking after it till Matt gets back."

"I see! Well, make sure you keep the little animal nice and warm." Cook glanced at the cookies in Scarlett's hand and smiled. "And if you need more cookies after you've finished those then I'll bake you a fresh batch!"

Scarlett beamed. "Thanks! I think your cookies are the best ones I've ever tasted."

As the three girls hurried upstairs, Zina added, "Your cook is really nice."

"She's lovely," Lily agreed, opening her bedroom door. "But I wish I'd done the ninja moves properly. It was all going well until my shoe squeaked. I don't think I'm ever going to be good at them." She sighed.

"I can help you!" Scarlett's eyes gleamed. "I haven't shown you the scissor jump move yet." She made a huge leap across the bedroom.

"Shh!" said Zina, with a warning look at Fudge, who was fast asleep.

Lily set the milk jug down and sank on to a chair. "I don't know if it would make much difference."

"But Rescue Princesses never give up!" Scarlett put her hands on her hips. "We can start right now if you want."

"Maybe we can find something else that will help you with your ninja moves," Zina's brow wrinkled thoughtfully, "like practising movements on a trampoline."

"I've got an even better idea." Scarlett smiled as she pressed her heart-shaped ruby ring. The jewel glowed brightly. Then Lily's sapphire ring and Zina's diamond ring lit up too. "I think we should make a new magic jewel!"

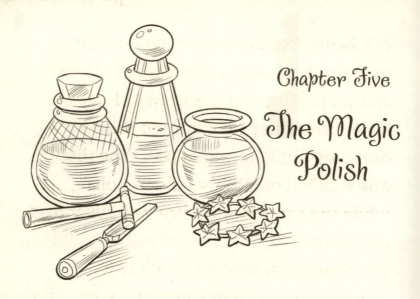

Chapter Five

The Magic Polish

Lily gazed at her glowing sapphire ring.
Her stomach did a somersault as she
thought about the magic inside. It would
be so exciting to make a new magic jewel.
"Did you bring the special jewel-making
tools in your suitcase, Scarlett?"

"Course I did!" Scarlett dashed out of
the room, returning a minute later with
a small wooden box. Inside was a tiny
set of chisels and a little silver hammer.
"Ever since we became Rescue Princesses

I've been doing as much jewel-making as I can. My cousin, Ella, sent me these special polishes too." She pulled out a little drawer in the bottom of the box and took out three glass pots. The first one was full of glittery golden polish, while the second and third had silver and orange polish.

"What do those do?" asked Lily.

"Ella told me the golden one is for friendship, the silver is for wishes and the orange one is for finding lost things. I used the gold pot when I made our magic rings. I just cut the jewels into a heart shape and rubbed a little polish on each of them." Scarlett smiled proudly.

"You did a great job!" said Zina, touching her diamond ring.

"Thanks!" Scarlett looked at Lily seriously. "Don't forget you have to choose the jewel you like best."

41

Lily opened her jewellery box and searched until she saw something that made her heart skip a beat – a beautiful bracelet made from pink crystal stars. "What do I do next, Scarlett?"

"Choose a polish and rub a little on each jewel." Scarlett's eyes gleamed.

Lily put on the bracelet and studied the pots of polish one by one. At last she chose the silver pot, the one for wishes. She smeared a little polish on each crystal. Then she closed her eyes for a moment. *I wish I was better at ninja skills...*

Zina gasped. "Lily, look!"

Lily opened her eyes again. The silver polish had started shimmering. Then little by little the polish disappeared, leaving the crystals brighter than before!

"Try a ninja move!" said Zina excitedly. "We won't look."

Lily left the room and waited till Scarlett

and Zina had turned away. Then she slipped back in, feeling as though she was full of fizzy lemonade! Her feet hardly seemed to touch the ground and she stopped right behind her friends, smiling.

"Lily, are you coming in?" called Scarlett.

"I'm here!" Lily said, laughing.

Zina and Scarlett spun round.

"I didn't know you were there!" gasped Scarlett. "The polish really worked then."

"I feel so much more *ninja* with the bracelet on," explained Lily. "I can do everything more smoothly."

"That's amazing!" said Zina.

"Can I have a go at wearing it?" asked Scarlett.

Lily handed the bracelet to Scarlett. "Thanks for helping me, Scarlett. I think this bracelet will come in very handy!"

💚

When Fudge woke up, she wriggled inside the bag and squeaked crossly.

"Do you think she's tired of being in there?" said Zina anxiously. "Maybe we should take her out for a while."

Lily lifted Fudge out of the bag and sat down with the joey on her lap. The little kangaroo wriggled more than ever. "Do you want to get down, Fudge?" She put the baby kangaroo on the floor.

Fudge's eyes brightened. She looked around and then did a few wobbly jumps across the room. Stopping beside Scarlett, she nibbled gently at the princess's skirt.

Scarlett giggled. "Stop it, Fudge. Your nose is tickly!"

Fudge straightened up and flexed her back legs as if she wanted to jump higher.

"Look, she's trying to hop properly," cried Lily. "Good try, Fudge." She knelt down and stroked the joey's soft ears.

"If she's fed up of being inside the bag then we need another way of carrying her around." Zina pushed her long dark hair over her shoulder. "And she needs to feel safe – just like she would in her mother's pouch." She hurried out of the room and came back with a fluffy yellow jumper. "Do you think she'd feel cosy under this jumper? You try it, Lily."

Lily pulled on the jumper. Then she slipped Fudge underneath, letting the little kangaroo's head poke out of the top. Fudge looked surprised for a moment, then she bleated happily. Lily smiled. "I think she likes it and she'll definitely stay warm."

Zina took a belt from Lily's wardrobe. "If you tie this round your waist then she won't slip out the bottom."

"Thanks, Zina!" Lily did up the belt and slipped the magical star bracelet into her

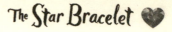

pocket. She felt a bit hot with the jumper on, but Fudge seemed comfortable. "Let's put up the posters for our cake sale and then we can get on with baking the cakes."

The sun came out from behind a cloud as the princesses stuck their posters to the royal gates. It was a busy street as the palace was close to the middle of the town, so people stopped to read the posters straightaway.

Lily grinned at the others, an excited, tickly feeling in her stomach. Soon lots of people would know about the cake sale. "Now we just have to make the cakes!" she told the others.

As the girls hurried back across the garden, Lily noticed a gleaming black car parked by the front door. "I wonder why Lady Hamilton's here again. She doesn't usually visit two days in a row."

"I hope she asks her driver to go more carefully this time," said Scarlett darkly.

Lily bit her lip. Maybe Lady Hamilton had come to say sorry for frightening the mother kangaroo yesterday. She took Fudge out of her jumper and handed the little kangaroo and the sweater to Zina. "I'm going to find out why she's here. I'll meet you in the kitchen."

Zina put on the jumper and settled Fudge comfortably. Lily tiptoed to the parlour door and listened for voices.

"But, Sarah, I'm sure it won't be as bad as you think," Queen Caroline was saying.

"It will be terrible!" cried Lady Hamilton. "The noise ... the smell... It'll make living in this area a nightmare."

Lily frowned. What were they talking about? What was going to be terrible?

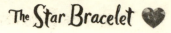

Taking the star bracelet out of her pocket, she slipped it on to her wrist. At once, every move she made felt smooth and perfect, like a swan gliding across a lake. Tiptoeing into the room, she ducked neatly behind an armchair. Lady Hamilton and the queen didn't even look up.

Lady Hamilton was sitting on the edge of her chair, fidgeting with her pearl necklace. Her face was flushed.

The queen took a sip of tea. "Perhaps if you had the chance to speak to Matt you'd see there's nothing to worry about."

"I'm sorry, Your Majesty, but I know that opening a kangaroo sanctuary around here would be a complete disaster!" Lady Hamilton's eyes were stern. "I'm determined to stop it happening and I demand that you help me."

49

Lily put her hand to her mouth. Why would Lady Hamilton want to stop the kangaroo sanctuary from opening? Without it, there would be no safe place for Fudge to grow up. Lily fiddled with the star bracelet and it fell off. Scrambling to pick it up, she bumped into a cupboard and made it rattle.

"What was that?" Lady Hamilton stared around.

After sliding the bracelet back on to her wrist, Lily tried not to move or even breathe.

"Never mind!" Lady Hamilton smoothed her dress. "As soon as I discovered that this kangaroo park would be right next door to my house, I knew I couldn't allow it to happen. The kangaroos will break out of that place! They'll squash the flowers and chew on the fences. It's inexcusable!"

"I understand it must have been a surprise," said the queen. "But I think having somewhere for lost kangaroos to go is a very good thing. We have to look after our Estaland animals, especially the baby ones."

"They're nothing but pests!" Lady Hamilton rose to her feet and picked up her handbag. "I heard of a place where kangaroos squashed every plant in the garden. That could happen here if you let those awful creatures bounce around everywhere. I think you'll be very sorry you didn't listen to me, Your Majesty. Goodbye!"

Lily shrank back into her hiding place as Lady Hamilton swept from the room. Her mum sighed and took another sip of tea. Lily crept out of the parlour and took off the star bracelet as she hurried to the kitchen.

Scarlett was at the kitchen table, weighing out the flour and the sugar while Zina searched for a mixing bowl. Fudge had fallen asleep again inside Zina's fluffy jumper.

Lily explained what Lady Hamilton had said. "She's determined not to let the sanctuary open, but if it doesn't all the poor kangaroos will have nowhere to go."

"That's awful!" cried Zina. "She can't stop the sanctuary opening, can she?"

Lily curled her hair behind her ear. "I don't know. I think she's cross because it'll be close to her house."

Scarlett stirred the eggs fiercely. "She can't stop us! We'll make the best cakes ever and raise lots of money – enough for twenty kangaroo sanctuaries."

Lily smiled. "You're right – we can't let her spoil everything. Pass me the butter and I'll start mixing!"

Chapter Six

Twenty-four Kinds of Cake

The girls added sugar, butter and eggs and mixed them carefully. They looked up dozens of recipes in the queen's royal cookery books. They put chocolate in some of the cakes and lemon in others. Once they'd made twelve batches of cupcakes, they baked some muffins and five trays of brownies.

Zina, who was still carrying Fudge, had to put the joey down when she awoke as she kept trying to lick the wooden spoon.

Fudge did some baby kangaroo hops round the kitchen, her feet hardly leaving the ground. She sniffed at the flour and ate half a packet of chocolate chips before Scarlett rescued them.

Cook came back in time to put the cake trays in the oven. When the cakes were cool enough, the girls mixed up icing in a rainbow of colours. On top of the iced cakes, they added butterfly decorations and tiny jelly sweets.

"My goodness!" said Cook. "I've never seen so many cakes on one table."

"There are twenty-four different kinds." Lily wiped her hands on her apron. "I counted them!"

"I wish we could try some," said Scarlett longingly. "Look at those ones with the white chocolate icing and strawberries on top. I bet they taste awesome!"

Lily gazed at the mountain of mixing

bowls and the table covered in flour. "We must have been cooking for hours! Let's clear up and then have a picnic lunch outside."

"I'll wash up – I'm good at it!" Scarlett poured water into the sink before adding big squirts of washing-up liquid.

Lily and Zina dried the bowls and spoons that Scarlett washed. Fudge began to squeak, and only settled down when Zina gave her another bottle of milk.

"What a sweet little kangaroo!" Cook handed Lily a picnic basket. "Here you are. I've made you some sandwiches and there are crisps and apples in there too."

"Thank you!" Lily took a picnic rug from the cupboard and the princesses trooped into the garden.

The sun was beaming down and a blue-feathered parrot watched them from the top of a tree. Lily led them down a path on to a wide stretch of grass and spread out the rug. "We can have the picnic here." She set the basket down and took out the cups and plates. Zina put Fudge onto the grass beside her.

"Lily, is your mother all right?" asked Zina suddenly.

Lily turned to look. The queen was standing very still beside a flowerbed and staring at the ground. She put a hand to her forehead and sighed.

Lily hurried over to her mum. "Is it all right if we have a picnic—" She stopped, noticing some rows of squashed bluebells.

The queen fixed her eyes on Lily. "Have you girls been playing around here? Did you tread on this flowerbed?"

Lily's mouth dropped open. "No, we didn't, I promise! We've been in the kitchen baking cakes."

The queen nodded. "I was sure you

wouldn't have done it. But oh ... my beautiful royal bluebells ... and the lilies have been trampled too. The only flowerbed that hasn't been damaged is the one with the roses near the golden wattle trees."

Lily's heart sank. She'd always loved lilies because she was named after them. Now their stalks were bent and the bright-pink petals were scattered across the earth. Only a few lilies were still standing.

It seemed strange that the flowers left upright were dotted round the border. What could have flattened some flowers completely but left others alone?

"Lady Hamilton was right." The queen picked up a crushed bluebell. "It must have been kangaroos that caused all this damage. She warned me that they can ruin gardens. Look at how the creature

has bounced on some flowers but not on others."

"I didn't see any kangaroos here when we came out of the kitchen," said Lily.

"What about the kangaroo that Matt was looking after? When he returns tomorrow I'll be having a serious talk with him about that creature." The queen's hand tightened round the broken bluebell. "Perhaps Lady Hamilton was right about the kangaroo sanctuary too. I'm beginning to think I shouldn't allow one to open around here after all."

Chapter Seven

The Broken Petals

Lily searched for the right words. She wanted to tell her mum that kangaroos couldn't have done all this damage. She wanted to say they were lovely animals that just needed a place where they'd be safe. But what if it *was* kangaroos that had flattened all the flowers?

Queen Caroline walked back into the palace, still holding the squashed bluebell. Zina and Scarlett came over to join Lily.

"What's wrong, Lily?" asked Zina, holding tight to Fudge.

"My mum thinks it was kangaroos that did all this to the flowerbed." Lily twisted a lock of hair around her finger. "She says maybe there shouldn't be a kangaroo sanctuary near here after all. But I don't understand – we've never had problems like this before!"

"Maybe the mother kangaroo came back to look for Fudge." Zina stroked the joey, whose sweet brown eyes were peeping out of the top of her jumper.

Lily shook her head. "The mothers never come back. Matt told me that once … and I don't think Hoppley could have done so much damage by himself."

"Hoppley was asleep in the stables this morning. I'm going to check if he's still there." Scarlett ran off.

Lily's mind was spinning as she knelt

down on the rug and took food out of the picnic basket. They'd spent hours baking for their cake sale but if her mum changed her mind about the kangaroo sanctuary there would be no point in having the sale at all.

"Don't worry," said Zina. "I'm sure we can prove it wasn't a kangaroo. Are there any other animals that squash plants?"

Lily shook her head. "I can't think of any." She handed out the sandwiches. They looked delicious but suddenly she felt too worried to be hungry.

Scarlett raced up and sank on to the picnic rug. "Hoppley's still sleeping on a hay bale and he doesn't look like he's moved. I don't think he did anything wrong!"

Zina bit into an apple. "Someone's outside the gate, Lily. Is it Matt? I thought he was coming back tomorrow."

Lily scrambled up and looked through a gap in the fence. "No, I think that's Lady Hamilton's car. I wonder why she's parked out there. She left here hours ago." Putting down her sandwich, she crept over to the gate.

The posh black car was parked on the other side of the road with the front window half open.

"I can't see anyone inside," whispered Scarlett, who had followed her. "Shall we use ninja moves to get a bit closer?"

"I'll go!" said Lily. "I won't be long." Putting on her star bracelet, she slipped lightly across the lawn as if her feet hardly touched the ground.

The driver, Delby, was pacing up and down beside the car with a phone to his ear. Lily waited till he turned away before tiptoeing through the palace gate and sliding behind a nearby bush.

Safe in her hiding place, she touched the star bracelet gently. With the help of a little magic, ninja moves had become easier than ever!

"Yes, most of it's done, My Lady," Delby said into the phone. "Shall I come back now?" He swung round and Lily froze. He must be talking to Lady Hamilton. But what did he mean – *most of it's done*?

Delby carried on pacing while Lily watched him from behind the bush. "No, My Lady, the princesses are in the garden so I can't go back right now. I'll return and finish off tonight." He pressed a button on the phone and put it in his pocket. As he climbed into the car, something pink dropped off the bottom of his shoe.

After he'd driven away, Lily climbed out of her hiding place. Crouching down, she studied the scraps of pink on the ground.

Her stomach tumbled over and over. She knew what they were. Lily petals!

Scarlett and Zina came running out. "Did you find out why Lady Hamilton's driver was here?" said Scarlett breathlessly.

Lily picked up the bits of torn petal. "These came off his shoe. He must have stepped on the flowers and bits of petal got stuck to his heels. That means he was the one that ruined the flowerbeds ... and I bet Lady Hamilton told him to!"

When Lily rushed inside to tell her mum about Lady Hamilton's driver, the queen cut her off. "That's enough, Lily! I'm sure nobody spoiled the garden on purpose. I know you don't want it to be true but I really think it must have been kangaroos."

Tears pricked Lily's eyes as she left the

parlour. Scarlett and Zina were waiting for her outside.

"Come on!" whispered Zina, putting an arm round her. "Let's go and talk in your room."

They went up to Lily's bedroom and Zina put Fudge down on the floor as she was wriggling so much. The little kangaroo flexed her legs and managed a baby hop.

"Go on, Fudge. Try jumping higher!" said Scarlett.

Fudge did three little jumps in a row to reach the window. Then she stopped and nibbled the end of the curtain.

"She seems to be getting stronger all the time," said Zina.

Lily smiled at the joey. "Well done, Fudge! At least no one can blame you for the ruined flowers." She sighed. "I'm *sure* Delby spoilt those flowerbeds but my mum thought I was being silly when I told her."

"It must be Lady Hamilton's plan for stopping the kangaroo sanctuary," said Scarlett. "She's made your mum think kangaroos are nothing but trouble!"

"It's really unfair!" Lily's cheeks went pink. "And the last thing the driver said was *I'll return and finish off tonight*."

"So he's planning to trample on the other flowerbeds too." Zina's eyes widened. "Then your mum will be so cross that she'll never want to see a kangaroo again!"

Scarlett's eyes gleamed. "But all we have to do is catch him damaging the garden. Then we'll have proof it wasn't a kangaroo at all."

"We'd have to take my mum outside to show her what he was doing," said Lily, frowning, "And I think she'd tell us off

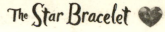

for being awake so late and make us go to bed. Unless ... maybe we could take a picture!"

"That's brilliant!" Scarlett jumped up so suddenly that Fudge squeaked and hid behind the curtain. "I brought a camera from home to take pictures of Estaland. We can use that!"

"Do you think we'll get close enough to take a picture?" said Zina.

Scarlett grinned. "We'll do some extra-awesome ninja moves and sneak in really close!"

Lily's tummy tingled as she thought about slipping out in the dark to catch Lady Hamilton's driver in the garden. It was a bit scary... but she couldn't let anyone get away with blaming the poor kangaroos for something they didn't do!

Chapter Eight

Adventure in the Dark

Scarlett and Zina put on their very best dresses for dinner that evening as Lily had told them they always dressed up when there were visitors. Scarlett wore a dark-green dress. A gold tiara with emeralds rested on top of her dark curly hair. Zina wore a long white dress and a silver tiara dotted with diamonds. She walked gracefully, holding the hem of her dress in one hand.

Lily's best dress was pale blue with a

long skirt stretching down to her ankles. She loved the way it floated as she walked but it did get in the way of running sometimes. Her silver tiara, which was decorated with pearls, had an annoying trick of slipping down her forehead. But she was too busy thinking about kangaroos to notice her long dress or slippy tiara this time.

Queen Caroline smiled and talked about Estaland all the way through dinner. She didn't mention the ruined flowerbeds.

The girls tucked into beef burgers and veggie burgers served with Cook's special royal chips and a leafy green salad. Then there was ice cream for pudding topped with raspberries and chocolate sauce. They climbed the stairs after dinner feeling very full and excited about their plans for that evening.

"I'll get my camera." Scarlett's eyes shone. "Then we can go and find a place to hide in the garden!"

"Wait! We'll be seen too easily if we go out wearing these clothes," said Lily. "Especially you in that white dress, Zina."

Zina wrinkled her brow. "I don't have many dark clothes. Most of my dresses are white or yellow..."

"I have LOTS of black leggings," Scarlett told them. "I'd wear leggings every day if I could! Come to my room and I'll find them." Running into her bedroom, she started pulling things out of her suitcase. Socks, T-shirts and tiaras went flying in all directions.

"Didn't you unpack before dinner?" asked Zina, trying to tidy up the mound of clothes on Scarlett's floor. "I've hung all my things in the wardrobe."

"Oh no, I was too busy! Here you are."

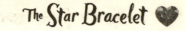

Scarlett handed Zina and Lily some leggings.

"Thanks!" said Lily. "Let's meet again in an hour. I don't think Lady Hamilton's servant will be here before dark."

Back in her room, Lily took off her best dress and tiara and put on the leggings with a dark-blue T-shirt. Fudge was still asleep, so she played with the star bracelet, putting it on and tiptoeing from one side of the room to the other. Then she leaned on the windowsill, watching the sky turn from sunset orange to dark blue and then to black. A bright full moon rose, turning the whole garden silver.

Lily thought about her mum. She hoped the queen wouldn't be cross with them for creeping outside when they were supposed to be in bed but she couldn't

73

think of any other way to prove that kangaroos hadn't damaged the garden.

There was a knock on the door and Scarlett came in. "Are you ready? Are you bringing Fudge?"

Lily stroked Fudge's ears. The joey's eyes were shut tight. "I think we should leave her here."

Scarlett nodded. "She might get upset if she's bumped around in the dark."

Lily slipped the star bracelet into her pocket and followed Scarlett, but as she reached the door Fudge squeaked. Then she twitched her ears and kicked against the cloth bag.

"What's wrong?" Lily stroked the little joey, trying to calm her down, but Fudge wriggled even harder.

Lily caught sight of some car headlights sweeping down the road beyond the palace fence. Lady Hamilton's servant

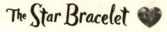

might be here at any moment. There was no time to lose. Picking up the bag with Fudge inside, she hung it carefully over her shoulder.

"Maybe she doesn't want to be left alone." Scarlett rubbed the joey's furry nose. "After all, she's only a baby."

They went to knock on Zina's door and then together the princesses crept downstairs to the hallway. Sneaking into the kitchen, Lily found two torches in a drawer and gave one to Zina and the other to Scarlett. Then she slid back the bolt on the door and tiptoed out into the moonlight.

The princesses waited for their eyes to get used to the dark. Strange night-time sounds poured over them – chirpings and squeaks and rustling in the trees.

Lily felt a prickle on the back of her neck. She knew the garden really well, she reminded herself. All the odd shapes in the dark were just trees and benches – things that looked quite normal in the daytime.

Scarlett nudged her. "Where shall we hide?"

"Over here!" Lily led them to the golden wattle trees. "This is the only flowerbed that didn't get damaged, so Delby is sure to come this way—" She broke off as Zina gave a shriek. "What is it?"

"There's something by that tree trunk – something big!" squeaked Zina.

A branch snapped. Two dark eyes gleamed in the torch beams. Then a brown furry animal the size of a pig sniffed the ground with its stubby nose before turning and trotting away.

"It's only a wombat!" said Lily, smiling. "You made me jump, Zina."

"It made *me* jump!" giggled Zina.

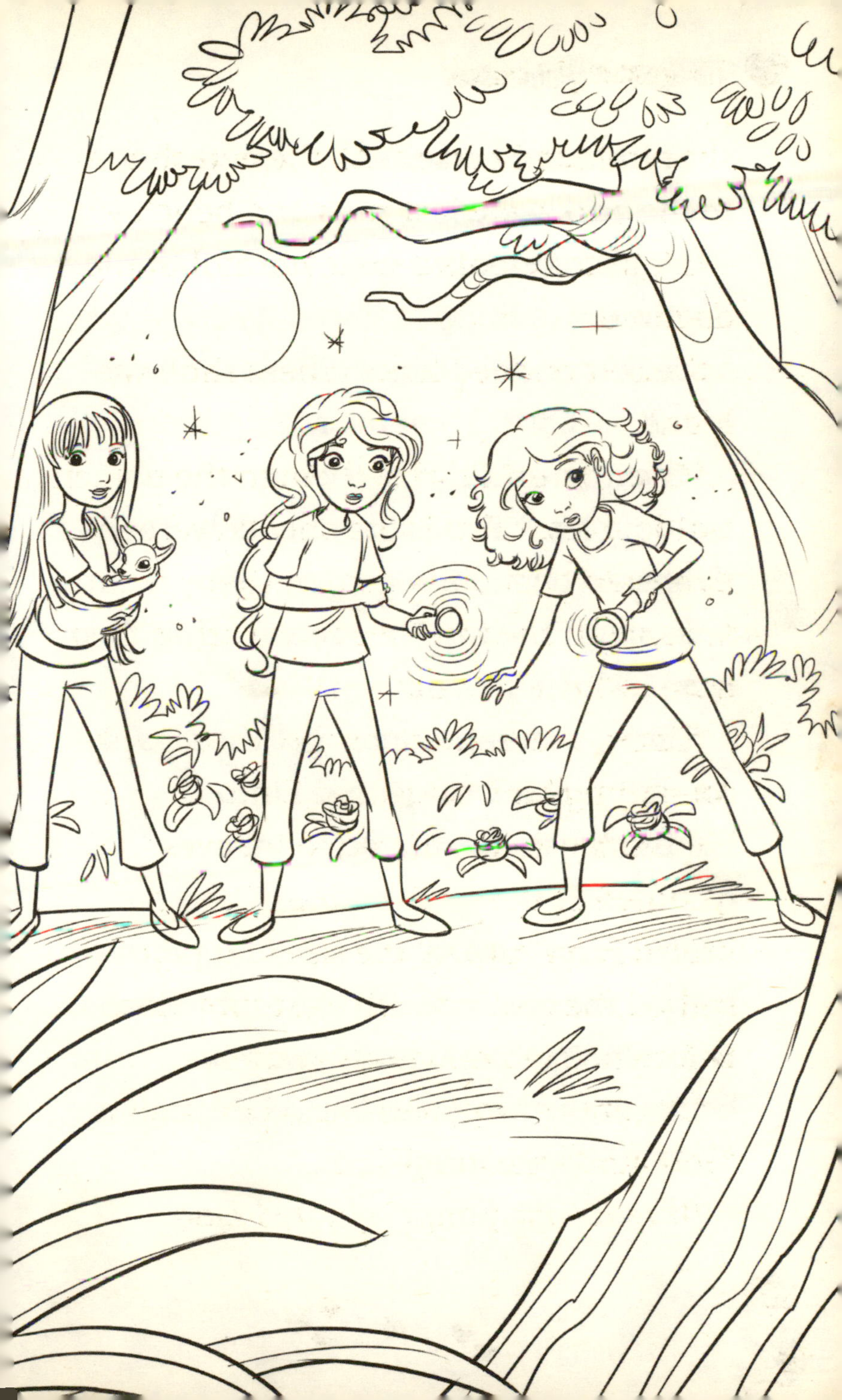

"Shh!" hissed Scarlett. "I can hear a car."

The princesses listened. The thrumming engine noise stopped and a stocky figure appeared at the palace gate and pulled at the padlock. Then the man gave up on the lock and climbed over the gate. Landing heavily on the other side, he lumbered across the garden.

"Turn off the torches. He's coming this way!" whispered Lily.

"Here – you'll probably get the closest." Scarlett pressed the camera into Lily's hands. "Push this button to take the picture."

Lily's heart raced. She slid a hand into her pocket and took out the star bracelet. Then she tiptoed forward, watching from between the branches and leaves.

Chapter Nine

Moonlight Trickery

As the dark figure came closer, Lily could see that it was Delby, Lady Hamilton's servant. He had a heavy frame and a round face, and he was puffing from the effort of climbing over the locked gate.

Lily crept to the edge of the clump of trees. Fudge kicked inside the bag and she quickly stroked the animal's fur to make her quiet.

Delby switched on a torch and swung the beam across the garden. Then he headed straight for the rose bushes that were bursting with beautiful red blooms. Lily slipped the star bracelet over her wrist. Her ninja moves had to be perfect. Heart thumping, she stepped out into the open.

Delby raised his foot over the flowerbed.

Lily slipped closer, keeping to the shadows. Then she lifted the camera to her eye, her finger ready on the button.

Stamping his foot, Delby broke the first rose stem. Then he crushed the rose petals under his boot.

Lily held her breath and pressed the button. There was a click and a light flashed on the camera.

Delby stumbled. "What...? Who's there?"

Lily put the camera in her pocket and looked around in panic. Where could she hide? Quickly, she dived behind a golden

wattle tree.

"Ouch!" Delby hooked his trousers away from the thorn and shone his torch right and left. Then he stopped with the beam fixed on Lily's hiding place. "Oh no! A giant kangaroo is following me!"

Lily's mouth dropped open. What was he talking about?

The man covered his eyes. "I'm sorry, kangaroo. I was only doing what My Lady told me to."

Lily looked down at Fudge, who was blinking in the bright torchlight. Suddenly she realised what was going on. She was hidden behind the tree, but Fudge was leaning forward and Delby must have spotted her. The torch beam cast a long shadow of Fudge's head, making her look much bigger than she really was!

While Delby was covering his eyes Lily

slipped back among the trees and took off the star bracelet. Scarlett squeezed her hand and whispered, "Did you get a good picture?"

"I think so," Lily whispered back. "Delby seems spooked out, doesn't he?"

Scarlett giggled, covering her mouth.

"It's disappeared!" moaned Delby, staring all around. "Who knows what's hiding in the shadows!"

Lily kept completely still. She hoped the man would be scared enough to go home. Fudge shuffled inside the bag and made a little bleating sound.

"What was that? It sounded more like a lamb than a grown kangaroo! There's some kind of moonlight trickery going on." Delby marched towards the trees where the girls were hiding.

"Everyone split up!" hissed Scarlett.

The princesses scattered in all

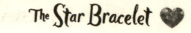

directions. Zina raced towards the back
door while Scarlett ran towards the
ruined flowerbeds. Lily dodged round
the side of the golden wattle trees, before
dashing towards the house.

"There you are!" cried Delby. "You're
just a baby kangaroo. It must have been
a trick of the light."

Lily swung round in horror. The bag at
her side suddenly felt very light. Where
was Fudge? Her heart dropped as she saw
Delby picking the joey up from the grass.
The little kangaroo struggled, her feet
kicking in the air.

Without stopping to think, Lily bravely
stepped out of the shadows. "Let her go!
I know you sneaked in here to damage
more plants."

Delby shone his torch right into her
eyes. "So it was you, Princess Lily ... and
you took a picture, didn't you? That's why

there was a flash. Give me that camera and you can have this little kangaroo back safe and sound." He smiled nastily and clutched the wriggling Fudge even tighter. "If you don't, you'll never see this animal again!"

Lily swallowed. Delby was even meaner than she'd thought!

There was the sound of running feet and Scarlett did a scissor jump over the nearest flowerbed. She landed on the other side and folded her arms. "You won't get away with this! We all saw what you did."

Delby just laughed. "Is that so? What exactly are you going to do then?"

"We'll tell the queen about it!" said Zina, dashing to Lily's side.

"And we'll make sure she knows that you flattened every flower you could find!" said Scarlett, and Zina nodded.

Lily's heart lifted. With the other Rescue Princesses to help, there was still a chance of getting Fudge back. Handing the bag to Scarlett, she whispered, "Keep him talking. I'm going to try some ninja moves!"

Scarlett nodded. "Hey!" She waved the bag at Delby. "I've got the camera if you really want it."

Delby charged at Scarlett with Fudge clutched under his arm. Scarlett darted away, springing over a flowerbed and escaping easily.

Lily slipped on her star bracelet. She felt a fluttering in her stomach. She only had one chance to get Fudge back so she would have to be very brave. Holding her breath she slipped through the shadows, determined not to let Delby get away.

Chapter Ten

A Wombat Surprise

Lily chased after Lady Hamilton's servant and the crystals on the star bracelet shimmered as she ran. Delby followed Scarlett halfway across the garden, then he stopped and bent over, wheezing.

Lily drew the camera from her pocket again. Maybe she could surprise Delby with another flash of light, giving her time to take Fudge back. She felt the bracelet helping her, steadying her feet and filling her with energy. She got the camera ready but, as she sneaked closer, something rustled in the undergrowth.

"What's that?" Delby looked around wildly. "That's it! I've had enough of all this." He marched back up the path with Fudge still under his arm. The little joey squeaked and struggled, so the man shook her crossly.

Lily's cheeks grew hot. How dare he treat Fudge like that?

Just as Delby marched past the trees, a huge wombat dashed in front of him. The man stepped sideways to avoid the creature but stumbled over a tree root and fell to his knees.

Lily leapt forward, raised the camera and pressed the button.

Snap! The camera light flashed and Delby put his hand over his eyes, letting Fudge slide to the ground.

The little joey jumped up, squeaking.

Lily scooped her up and ran. She kept on running – not looking back until she was inside the palace. Leaning against the kitchen table, she tried to get her breath back. Fudge nuzzled her shoulder.

"Lily, are you all right?" Zina came running in after her. "You were so quick – getting hold of Fudge like that."

"Thanks!" gasped Lily. "Where's Scarlett?"

"I saw her sneaking after Lady Hamilton's servant," replied Zina.

"She's following him?" Lily's eyes widened. "Then we should be able to see them from upstairs." Holding Fudge tight, Lily raced up the steps to her room and pulled back her curtain.

The moon shone brightly over the palace garden. It was easy to spot Delby lumbering towards the gate. A small figure slipped after him. Delby swung

round a few times, but Scarlett hid so well that he didn't see her.

A door swung open along the corridor. "Girls, what are you doing? You should be in bed by now." The queen came out of her room, wrapping a gold dressing gown around her. She frowned when she noticed Fudge. "Lily, why have you brought that animal in here?"

Lily's heart sank. "We found her this morning when she fell out of her mother's pouch. She's only a baby."

"I can see that but why is she here inside the palace and why are you wearing those odd clothes?" Queen Caroline sat down on Lily's bed and studied the girls' faces.

So Lily explained how Lady Hamilton's driver had beeped his car horn and scared the mother kangaroo and the baby had fallen out of her pouch.

She told her mum about the broken petals on the bottom of Delby's shoes and how they'd been sure that destroying the royal garden was a plot to change the queen's mind about the kangaroo sanctuary.

"So we went outside to see if Lady Hamilton's servant would come back." Lily handed the camera to the queen. "And I got a picture of him."

Queen Caroline pressed a button to bring up the pictures. Delby was caught in the camera flash with his boot squashing the roses. The queen's face darkened like a storm cloud. "Well! I talked very politely to Lady Hamilton about the kangaroo sanctuary and instead of being reasonable she goes behind my back and sends a servant to ruin my beautiful garden. This is very disappointing indeed!"

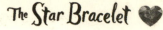

Scarlett rushed in. "It's OK! The man's gone and—" She broke off, noticing the queen sitting on Lily's bed.

Queen Caroline stood up and gently stroked Fudge's ears. "I'm sorry I didn't listen to you earlier, Lily. You may keep the little kangaroo in here tonight but tomorrow Matt must take care of him." She smiled. "Now, off to bed. You've all had enough excitement for one night!"

"Your mum's really nice," said Zina after the queen had gone. "I'm glad she knows we're telling the truth now."

"That man won't sneak in here again," said Scarlett, yawning. "He wouldn't dare!"

"And Fudge is safe," said Lily. "That's the most important thing of all!" She took the star bracelet out of her pocket and laid it on her bedside table. The pink crystals shone gently in the light.

Lily smiled. Her ninja moves had improved so much – with a little magical help – that she hardly needed the bracelet any more.

In the morning, the queen called the princesses down to breakfast. Lily left Fudge sleeping in the cloth bag and hurried downstairs, her stomach rumbling. Zina and Scarlett were waiting in the dining room.

"After your adventures last night I thought you might be hungry." The queen pointed to the dishes piled high with sausages, eggs and bacon. "So I asked Cook to make you a large breakfast."

A shiny black car slid up the drive. Lily paused halfway through spooning sausages on to her plate. Was that Lady Hamilton?

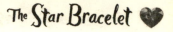

"Now, please excuse me, as I have something important to attend to." Queen Caroline swept out of the dining room.

Lily watched as the car stopped at the front steps. Delby got out and hurried round the side to open Lady Hamilton's door. "What are *they* here for?"

Lady Hamilton marched up the palace steps with a snooty look on her face.

Scarlett raised her eyebrows. "Lady Hamilton doesn't look like she's come to apologise."

Lily crept to the door. "I hope she doesn't blame everything on the kangaroos again."

"She'd better not!" Scarlett set her knife and fork down and followed Lily to the door. Zina hurried after them and the three princesses tiptoed up to the parlour door and listened.

95

"But, Sarah," the queen was saying. "The princesses saw him in the garden. They even took a picture to show me what he was doing."

"I'm so sorry, Your Majesty!" said Delby. "I'll do anything I can to put it right..."

"Be quiet, Delby!" snapped Lady Hamilton. "The point is it *could* have been kangaroos and I knew I had to open your eyes to what might happen if you let the horrible beasts live close by."

"By ruining my garden!" The queen's voice rose. "That's not what a good friend should do."

"Why were the princesses running round the garden at night, anyway?" replied Lady Hamilton. "It sounds like they need some training in good manners and proper royal behaviour!"

"Lily and her friends are brave and capable girls who care about animals,"

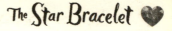

snapped the queen. "They don't need any training at all. You may leave now and don't *ever* return here again."

The princesses jumped behind the dining-room door as Lady Hamilton swept from the room.

"The queen really told her off!" Scarlett whispered gleefully.

"And she called us brave!" said Zina.

The front door banged and the princesses crept back into the hallway. Lily caught a glimpse of Delby kneeling before the queen through a crack in the parlour door.

"You can get up now, Delby," said the queen. "And if you really *are* sorry and you mean what you say about putting things right, then I have lots of gardening for you to do."

Chapter Eleven

A Royal Cake Sale

Lily, Scarlett and Zina added a note to their posters, saying that the cake sale would begin at 12 o'clock. Then they dashed to the kitchen to add more decorations to the cakes, like coloured sprinkles and icing swirls. Fudge woke up and explored the kitchen, getting into the cupboards and knocking over the saucepans.

Scarlett wrote down the prices of the cakes, muffins and brownies on some special gold labels. Then Lily and Zinu loaded the cakes on to silver trays and took them out into the garden. Cook set up two wooden tables just inside the palace gates and Lily covered each one with a lacy white tablecloth. By the time they'd finished arranging the cakes and the labels, a small crowd had begun to gather.

"I'd like to buy four brownies, please," said a dad with a small boy. "We'll take them home and have them after dinner."

"Here you are!" Lily put the brownies in a paper bag and handed them over, smiling. Then she took the money and gave the man his change.

The next customer asked for butterfly cakes and the next wanted blueberry muffins. Soon all the princesses were handing out cakes and taking money as more and more people came by.

Lily carried Fudge for a while to make sure she didn't get lost in the crowd. Lots of people came to meet the little joey and said what a good idea it was to raise money for a kangaroo sanctuary.

A man in a baseball cap was the last person in the queue. "Wow, these look delicious! I'm lucky there are any cakes left at all."

"Matt, you're back!" cried Lily, recognising him under the cap. "We've raised so much money for the kangaroo sanctuary ... and look at the joey we rescued."

"Thank you for doing all this, Princess Lily." Matt tickled the kangaroo under her chin. "And what's this little one called?"

"Fudge!" said the girls altogether.

💜

The next day, Matt drove the princesses

to the place where he was building his kangaroo sanctuary. Queen Caroline came with them so all the princesses squeezed into the back with Fudge.

Matt parked by a wooden gate. At the top of an overgrown path stood a big old house with a large stable beside it.

"It still needs a lot more work – especially the stables," said Matt, holding open the creaky gate. "But now we have the money from the cake sale, I think I can mend the stable roof and get everything ready for the kangaroos."

"It sounds as if you have it all planned out." The queen turned to Lily. "Why don't you and your friends get some fresh air while Matt shows me the house and stables."

Lily nodded. "I think Fudge would like to get out and explore." She was about to take the joey out of the bag but Scarlett

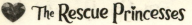

pulled her across the field.

"I can see a stream!" shouted Scarlett as she ran.

The air buzzed with insects and a pink-nosed, big-eared possum stared down at them from the top of a tree.

"Stop, Scarlett!" gasped Lily. "I can't run any more and I don't want to drop Fudge."

They stopped by the tiny, sparkling stream and Scarlett took off her shoes to paddle. Lily lifted Fudge out of the cloth bag and set her gently down on the grass. The kangaroo looked around. Her eyes brightened and she did a baby hop.

"Come on, Fudge!" coaxed Lily. "Try doing a bigger jump."

Fudge flexed her legs but her feet didn't leave the ground at all.

"She's not used to jumping high," said Zina.

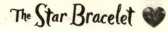

"But she's a kangaroo," Lily pointed out. "She must be able to do it!"

Fudge twitched her ears and squeaked eagerly.

"Fudge – jump!" said Lily softly. "You can do it!"

Scarlett waded out of the stream. "Maybe we should show her what to do. Fudge, watch this..." She leapt into the air.

Lily joined in with a really high leap. "Like this Fudge ... jump!"

Zina started bouncing too. "You can do it, Fudge!"

Fudge watched them, wide-eyed. Then she bent her legs and did a bigger hop.

"That's it!" Lily jumped even higher in excitement. "Well done, Fudge. Try another one."

Fudge hopped again and again, getting higher and higher each time. At last she

was bounding around the meadow, just like the princesses.

"She's getting the hang of it!" cried Lily.

Fudge squeaked with happiness as she followed the leaping princesses across the grass. At last they all grew tired. Lily sat down to get her breath back and Fudge curled up in her lap.

"This place will make a great kangaroo sanctuary," said Scarlett.

Lily stroked Fudge's ears. "You must come and visit me again when it's finished. Then you can see Fudge again too!"

"Yes, please!" Zina's eyes shone. "But first you must all come to my country, the Kingdom of Ramova. We have beautiful rainforests full of lizards, parrots, brightly coloured frogs and playful lemurs. I would like to show you everything!"

Lily's heart skipped. "I'd love to come to Ramova."

Zina smiled widely. "Next month there will be a carnival with costumes and music and dancing. I will ask my parents if you can both come and stay with us."

As Zina and Scarlett went on talking, Lily looked around and smiled happily. The sun shone warmly and parrots chattered in the trees. This place was going to be a happy home for all the lost kangaroos. She stroked Fudge's fur as the little joey fell asleep with her head resting on Lily's knee.

Look out for another
daring animal adventure!

The Rescue Princesses
The Shimmering Stone

Chapter One

The Royal
Wedding

Princess Amina tiptoed into the palace
courtyard and peered out from behind
a pillar, clutching her binoculars in one
hand. Her long black hair hung loosely
over her turquoise dress. On her arm
she wore a bracelet with a golden-brown
stone that shimmered as she moved.

She looked around carefully. Rows of
tables were laid out in the centre of the
courtyard, ready for the banquet tonight.
There was nobody here. If she was quick,

maybe she could reach the garden without being seen! She cast one last look around before darting out of her hiding place and running across the courtyard. She'd nearly reached the other side when she ran straight into her cousin, Princess Rani, and tumbled to the ground.

Rani, who was much older and taller, helped her up. "Hey!" she said, laughing. "What's the hurry? Is there a wild animal chasing you?"

"Oh, sorry, Rani! I didn't see you!" gasped Amina.

"Don't worry, I'm all right!" said Rani. "But why are you in such a rush?"

"I was looking out of the bedroom window with my binoculars and I'm sure I saw a tiger outside the palace wall!" explained Amina. "It was walking through the long grass beside the river. I was just going to take a closer look." She held out her binoculars. "Oh, no!" She stopped and looked at them more closely.

"What's wrong?" asked Rani.

"One of the lenses is broken. I must have knocked it against the ground when I fell over." She showed her cousin the crack in the glass on one side of the binoculars. Her heart sank. She used her binoculars nearly every day. They were so handy for seeing all the Kamalan wildlife.

"What a shame!" said Rani sympathetically. "I know how much you love them. Come and show me the tiger – we can close one eye and look through the side that isn't broken."

"All right then." Amina turned towards the archway that led out to the garden.

"Rani! Amina! Where are you?" A loud voice came from inside the palace.

Amina froze. Her aunt, Queen Keshi,

had been hurrying around the palace all morning. With the royal visitors due to arrive that day there was lots to do.

"Mum wants us," said Rani. "We'll have to look for your tiger later."

"But he might have gone by then!" Amina looked longingly at the archway. If only she could get through before her aunt came along. She wanted to see the tiger so much!

"You go, then," said Rani. "Mum probably wants me to try on my wedding dress for the hundredth time! You should go and have some fun."

Amina grinned. Even though Rani was much older, she was a perfect cousin – kind and funny. Amina was so happy that she was going to be her bridesmaid the next day!

"There you are!" Queen Keshi climbed down the steps to the courtyard, wearing a purple sari and a gold crown.

"Rani, you must try on your wedding dress one more time. Amina, I have some jobs for you to do. The royal guests are already starting to arrive and I am determined that this shall be the best wedding ever held in the Kingdom of Kamala!"

"But Aunt!" began Amina. "Could I go out into the garden first because—"

Queen Keshi waved her hands. "Amina! There isn't much time! We need to get the table decorations right and then we have to check that the guests' rooms are ready."

Amina's shoulders drooped. She wished she could go and see the tiger first. She'd seen deer and monkeys near the palace before, but never a tiger.

Rani noticed her disappointed face.

"Maybe Amina could pick some flowers

from the garden to decorate the tables?" she said. "Perhaps some of those pink and white lilies."

Amina perked up. If she was picking flowers in the garden, then she could sneak a look over the wall with her binoculars at the same time. She looked hopefully at her aunt.

Queen Keshi nodded. "Just make sure you pick plenty, and *don't* forget to put them in water so that they last until the wedding. And *don't* get dirt under your fingernails!" And she swept back up the steps.

Rani gave Amina a quick grin and followed her mum.

Amina hurried through the archway, grateful that Rani had found her a reason to be out in the garden. She was also glad that the queen hadn't noticed her binoculars as she would have wanted to know what Amina was up to.

She walked down to the side gate and climbed the stone steps that led up to the top of the high wall. There was a walkway there that the guards used when they were patrolling. Amina leaned her elbows on the stone and lifted the undamaged part of the binoculars to one eye.

The Palace of Kamala stood on top of a hill. The countryside spread out below, full of grass and rocks and bushes. A sparkling river wound its way through the middle and purple mountains rose in the distance.

Amina scanned the tall grass near the river. At first, she couldn't see the tiger and she began to wonder if it had disappeared among the bushes. Then a sudden movement caught her eye.

A large tiger with bold black stripes

walked proudly along the river bank and lifted its head to look around. It had a white mark on its nose.

For a moment, Amina wondered if she should have told her aunt about the tiger. Queen Keshi loved animals and had even set up a wildlife hospital on the far side of the palace grounds so that any sick animals could be cared for. But lately it had been difficult talking to her aunt because she was so busy thinking about Rani's wedding.

As Amina watched the beautiful tiger, she noticed a patch of long grass begin to quiver. Two more animals with orange and black stripes sprang out and galloped down the river bank. These tigers were *much* smaller. They chased each other playfully and tumbled over into the grass.

The Secret Rescuers

LOOK OUT FOR
THE JASMINE GREEN SERIES!

1

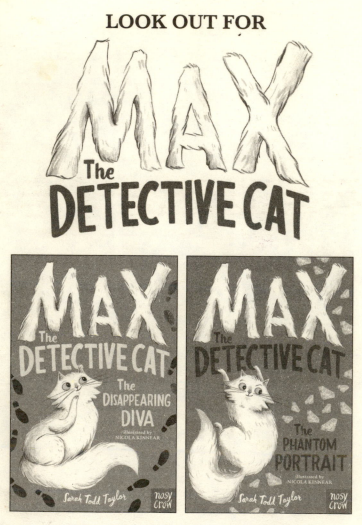